EX LIBRIS

THIS BOOK BELONGS TO:

WARNING! DO _NOT_ USE YOUR REAL NAME!

"THE TRUE SPY STORY RESEMBLES REAL LIFE AS WE ACTUALLY KNOW IT— A PLACE WHERE IT IS RARELY QUITE CLEAR WHAT IS HAPPENING AND WHAT ONE OUGHT TO DO."

— STELLA RIMINGTON

A NOTE ON THE ART

Astute readers may notice that sometimes an object described as having a certain color is shown in the pictures to have a different color. For instance, in this book there is an illustration of the Welsh flag that has a purple field and orange dragon. In real life, the flag has a green field and a red dragon. A sturgeon appears purple, although they're actually a disgusting greenish-gray slime color. My mom's boyfriend has an orange mustache, but he really had a *strawberry blond* mustache. That's because we only use three kinds of ink to print the artwork in this book: black, orange, and purple. So everything in this book, no matter what color it is in real life, looks black, orange, or purple. Or white! That's where we didn't use any ink at all. You probably didn't need a note explaining all this. We just didn't want you thinking we think Uranus is purple. We know it's blue. We take this *seriously.*

—M.B.

To Ms. Knox.
—M.B.

To my incredible parents, Jan and Steve.
—M.L.

Text copyright © 2019 by Mac Barnett • Illustrations copyright © 2019 by Mike Lowery
All rights reserved. Published by Orchard Books, an imprint of Scholastic Inc., *Publishers since 1920.* ORCHARD BOOKS and design are registered trademarks of Watts Publishing Group, Ltd., used under license. SCHOLASTIC and associated logos are trademarks and/or registered trademarks of Scholastic Inc. • Game Boy is a registered trademark of Nintendo Co. Ltd. • The publisher does not have any control over and does not assume any responsibility for author or third-party websites or their content. No part of this publication may be reproduced, stored in a retrieval system, or transmitted in any form or by any means, electronic, mechanical, photocopying, recording, or otherwise, without written permission of the publisher. For information regarding permission, write to Scholastic Inc., Attention: Permissions Department, 557 Broadway, New York, NY 10012. • This book is a work of fiction. Names, characters, places, and incidents are either the product of the author's imagination or are used fictitiously, and any resemblance to actual persons, living or dead, business establishments, events, or locales is entirely coincidental.

Library of Congress Cataloging-in-Publication Data available
ISBN 978-1-338-14371-3
10 9 8 7 6 5 4 3 2 1   19 20 21 22 23
Printed in China   62 • First edition, September 2019
The text type was set in Twentieth Century.
The display type was hand lettered by Mike Lowery.
Book design by Doan Buu

MAC B.

KID SPY

TOP SECRET SMACKDOWN

WITHDRAWN

By **Mac Barnett**

Illustrated by **Mike Lowery**

Orchard Books
New York
An Imprint of Scholastic Inc.

ME AS A ~~KID~~ SPY!

MY NAME IS MAC BARNETT. I AM AN AUTHOR. BUT BEFORE I WAS AN AUTHOR, I WAS A KID. AND WHEN I WAS A KID, I WAS A SPY.

AN AUTHOR'S JOB IS TO MAKE UP STORIES. BUT THE STORY YOU ARE ABOUT TO READ IS TRUE.

THIS ACTUALLY HAPPENED TO ME.

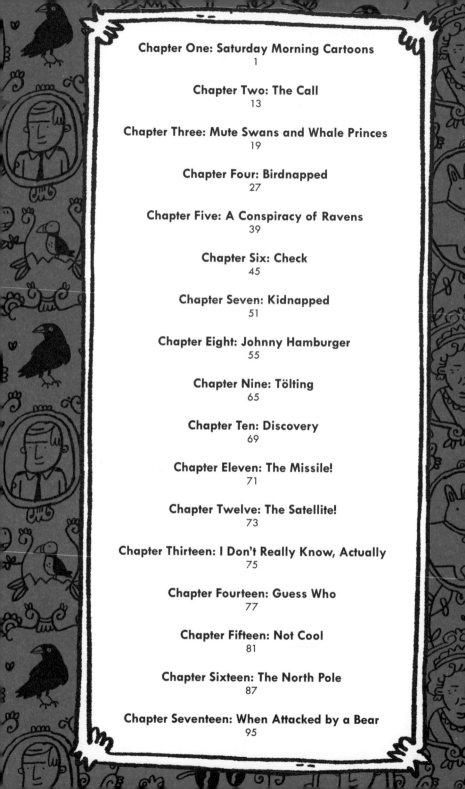

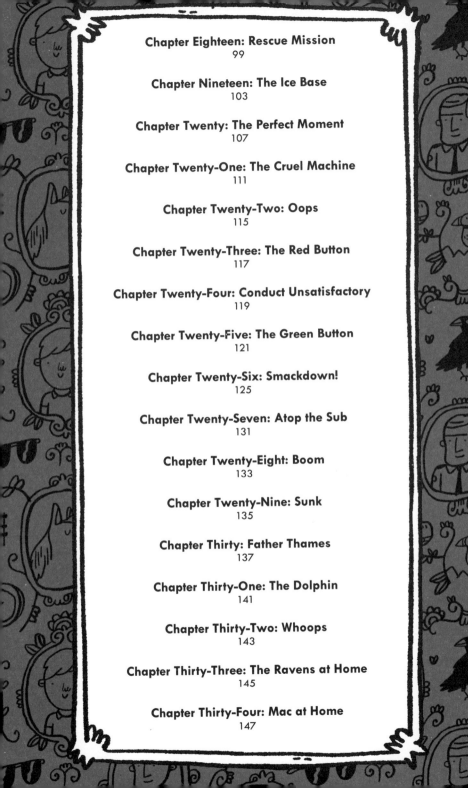

When I was a kid, I lived in California. (I still do.) California is a state on the very edge of the United States of America. I grew up in a little house with my mom and two rabbits. This is me when I was a kid.

ME

I was the shortest boy in my class, and shorter than most of the girls too. I'm taller now.

This is me and my mom.

Today she is about the same height.
This is me holding my rabbits, Maurice and Taylor.

Maurice and Taylor are not any size today,
because they are not alive. Pet rabbits live for

about ten years (that's true—you can look it up), and this story takes place a long time ago, all the way back in the 1980s.

OK:

It was Saturday. I woke up early. Usually on Saturday mornings, my mom's boyfriend, Craig, was camped out in front of the TV, watching WrestleFest. But Craig and my mom were in a fight, so I got to watch cartoons. I watched with the volume turned down low, so it didn't wake up my mom. I had to press my head up pretty close to the TV to hear it.

I ate a bowl of Trix—while watching a Trix commercial!

At noon, when the TV stations switched to sports and reruns, I went up to my room.

Then I got bored.

I usually got bored on Saturday afternoons. They seemed to stretch on for way too long. My mom was sitting at the kitchen counter, paying bills and making lists. She got annoyed if I distracted her. So I would stay up in my room and play Game Boy, until I got tired of Game Boy and switched to reading, until I got tired of reading and switched to action figures, then to stuffed animals, then to Matchbox cars, then Micro Machines (which were like tiny Matchbox cars), then back to Game Boy.

When I tiptoed out to check the time on the microwave, only forty-five minutes had passed!

"What are you doing?" my mom asked without looking up from her calculator. "Why are you sneaking around?"

"I'm tiptoeing," I whispered, "so I don't distract you."

"Why are you whispering?"

"So I don't distract you."

"It's distracting."

I went back up to my room. I lay on the floor, amid my toys and stuffed animals and books and Game Boy games, and just stared at the ceiling. I got so bored I screamed.

"Ahhhhhh!" I said.

"Are you OK?" my mom called from the kitchen.

"Yeah!" I said.

"You're being distracting."

"Ahhhhhh!" I said really quietly, so I didn't distract my mom.

And then the phone rang.

I jumped up.

Today, when I am writing this book, phones look like this:

If you are reading this book ten years from now, who knows what phones look like. Probably this:

But in the 1980s, they looked like this:

Whenever the phone rang, it was my job to run to the living room and answer it. I ran fast, and I was full of hope. If you've read the other books in this series, you know why: When I was a kid, sometimes the Queen of England would call me, out of the blue, and send me on an adventure. A dangerous adventure. A mysterious adventure. A spy adventure.

I picked up the phone.

"Hello?" I said.

It was not the Queen of England.

It was Craig.

"Julie? Hey, baby," said Craig.

(Julie was my mom's name. It still is.)

"Um," I said. "It's Mac."

"Oh! Mac! Hi, buddy! I thought you were your mom!"

"Yeah," I said.

"You kind of sound like her on the phone."

"OK," I said.

"Your voice is high, I guess."

"OK."

"Cuz you're just a kid."

"OK."

"Well listen, buddy, is your mom around?"

"No," I said.

My mom was around. She was in the kitchen, with her calculator. But she and Craig were in a fight, and part of my job answering the phone was "screening calls." Screening calls meant not putting her on the phone when she and Craig were having an argument.

"Your mom is not around."

"No."

"She's not home."

"Nope."

"Where is she?"

I named the first place I could think of.

"The donut shop."

"The donut shop."

"Yep. Rudy's."

(If you're ever in Castro Valley, California, you should go to Rudy's on Castro Valley Boulevard. Everything there is good, but they have a cinnamon donut that's shaped like a butterfly. It tastes great with milk, which they also sell at Rudy's.)

"Your mom went to Rudy's," Craig said, "and she just left you home alone."

"Yes."

"That doesn't sound like her."

Craig was right. That didn't sound like her.

"It was an emergency," I said.

"A donut emergency."

"Yes."

Craig sighed. "All right, budster. Hey! Listen, while I got you on the phone here, I was thinking we should spend some bonding time together!"

9

"Hmmm," I said. I had a feeling my mom was the one thinking Craig and I should spend some bonding time together.

"How about I get us a couple tickets to WrestleFest Live?" Craig said. "It's coming to town! Joe Brawn is gonna take down The Dictator!"

"Um," I said.

"You love WrestleFest!" said Craig.

"*You* love WrestleFest," I told Craig.

"You don't love WrestleFest?"

"Wrestling's fake," I said.

"No, it's real!" Craig said.

"No, they say it's real, but it's fake."

"I don't think you're right about that," Craig said.

"OK," I said.

"Well," said Craig. "Think about it. And tell your mom I invited you. And tell her I called. And tell her I'm really sorry, from the bottom of my heart. And tell her I love her, and she can call me back whenever she feels like it. I'm at the firehouse."

"OK."

Craig hung up.

"Who was it?" my mom said.

"Craig!"

There was no way I was giving her the rest of that message.

"Hmmm," my mom said.

I placed the phone back in the cradle.

As soon as I did, it rang again.

It was the Queen of England.

"Hello?" I said.

"Hullo," said the Queen of England. "May I please speak to Mac?"

"Speaking," I said.

"Mac! What is happening over there? I have been trying to get through to you for ages."

"Ages?"

"Three minutes, at least. Your line was engaged."

In the 1980s, phones could only handle one call at a time.

"Sorry. I was talking to my mom's boyfriend."

"Craig?" said the Queen. "Why were you talking to Craig? If I am correct, Craig is not particularly fond of you."

"You are correct. He and my mom are in a fight."

"Oh?" said the Queen. "About what? No! Never mind. This is no time for idle gossip, Mac. There is an urgent mission I must discuss with you. The matter at hand is both grave and consequential."

There was a click, and somebody started dialing. *Boop beep beep boop.*

"What is that?" the Queen asked. "What is going on?"

"I think somebody else is on the line," I said.

"Is it your mother?" asked the Queen. "Is she calling Craig back? To apologize? Are they going to get married?"

"What? No. My mom is paying bills in the kitchen."

There was more dialing. *Boop beep beep.* Then there was some splashing, and finally a man said, "Hullo?"

"Hullo?" said the Queen.

"Hullo!" said the man. "I'd like to order a medium pizza, sausage, onions—"

"Dear," said the Queen.

"Mummy?" said the man. "Mummy, what are you doing answering phones at a pizza parlor?"

"I am on a top secret call, dear. You picked up the spy phone again."

"Oh," said the man. "Which one is the regular phone?"

"The gold one."

"They're both gold, Mummy. Every phone in this palace is gold!"

"Where are you now, dear?"

"I'm in the bath!"

"The phone on the right, then. With the mother-of-pearl handle."

"Right-o!"

"And dear?" said the Queen. "Order a large pizza. It is a better value."

"That's true," I said, mostly because I hadn't said anything in a while.

The man hung up.

"Who was that?" I asked.

"That was my son," said the Queen. "The Prince of Wales."

"You must have a really big bathtub!" I said.

"Excuse me?" said the Queen.

"Um," I said, "you know. Like, Prince of Whales. W-H-A-L-E-S? Whales? So, you must have a really big bathtub?"

I could tell the Queen was frowning, even over the phone.

"Wales," said the Queen. "No 'h.'"

"Right," I said.

"Wales is a country, Mac. It is part of the United Kingdom."

"OK."

"The United Kingdom, of which I am the Queen, encompasses four countries: England, Scotland, Northern Ireland, and Wales."

"Oh boy."

"My son's royal title is the Prince of Wales. He is not a whale. That is absurd."

"Yeah, it was just a joke."

"Mac," said the Queen, "I am of the firm belief that jokes should be funny."

"Oh."

"In any case, yes, our bathtub is enormous."

"OK."

"But enough about bathtubs! Mac, I have called you because I need a favor. I am in the middle of a national emergency!"

"Wow!" I said.

"Yes. I am afraid the situation is quite dire."

The phone clicked and someone started dialing again.

"Hullo?" said a man. "I'd like to order a large pizza, sausage, onions——"

"Mac, perhaps you should just come over here so that we may speak in person. I shall send a helicopter."

That's how it happens. One minute you are lying bored on the floor of your bedroom, the next you are boarding a helicopter, which takes you to a spy plane (a regular plane with a spy on it, me) that flies you to the United Kingdom. It may seem strange that life can change so fast, but life is strange and always changing, even if you're not a spy. And I *was* a spy. So my life was very strange.

This is the United Kingdom:

The Queen was in Buckingham Palace, which is in London, which is in England, which, as you know, is in the UK (unless you didn't know that the UK is short for the United Kingdom—but if you didn't, now you do!).

I found the Queen sitting on a throne, with a large swan on her lap.

"Oh," I said.

"Yes?" The Queen smoothed the swan's feathers.

"Is that your swan?" I asked.

"Of course it is," said the Queen. "They're all mine."

"All the . . ."

"All the swans. I own any and all mute swans swimming in open waters in this country."

"Mute swans?" I asked.

"Yes," said the Queen. "It is a kind of swan. This is a mute swan."

The swan honked loudly.

"Not a great name," I said.

The Queen frowned. "Don't listen to him, Hugh," she said.

"Do you really own all the swans?" I asked. "That seems made up."

"It is true," said the Queen. "The Crown has owned all the swans in Britain for nine hundred years. You can look it up."

"Um, maybe I will when I get home."

(I did. It was true.)

"I also own every sturgeon, dolphin, and porpoise in British waters," said the Queen. "Do you know the difference between a dolphin and a porpoise?"

"Is this a joke?" I asked.

"No," said the Queen.

"It sounds like a joke."

"It is not a joke!" said the Queen. "I wouldn't make a joke about my porpoises!"

"OK," I said. "What's the difference?"

"It's all in their smiles," the Queen said. "Dolphins have long beaks and cone-shaped teeth, but porpoises have flatter faces and teeth like little shovels. And dolphins are chattier."

"Chattier?"

"Yes," said the Queen. "They even talk through their blowholes."

"Um," I said.

"And don't even get me started on my whales," said the Queen.

"You own all the whales too?"

"Of course," said the Queen.

I grinned. "I guess that makes you the Queen of Whales."

The Queen stared at me.

Her swan, Hugh, also stared at me.

"Get it," I said, "like the Prince of Wales?"

"Oh, I get it," said the Queen. "You are lucky I am English, and not Welsh, which is what you call someone from Wales. I simply do not find your joke funny. But a Welsh person might find it offensive."

"I don't think so," I said. "It's just a pun. Hey, why don't we ask your son! He's the Prince of Wales!"

The Queen grimaced. "My son is the Prince of Wales, but he is not Welsh."

"I feel like a Welsh person might find *that* offensive."

"Enough!" said the Queen. "You are wasting my time, and Hugh's. Mac, I need a favor from you." She leaned forward. "Someone has stolen something from the Tower of London!"

"Let me guess," I said. "The Crown Jewels."

"Let me finish," said the Queen. "No."

"Oh," I said. Usually, when the Queen asked me for a favor, someone had stolen the Crown Jewels. "What did they take, then?"

"Someone has stolen," said the Queen, "several birds!"

I gasped. "Swans?"

The Queen frowned. "Swans? No. Why would you think it was swans?"

I stared at the Queen.

"No reason, I guess," I said.

"This is much bigger than swans, Mac. But also much smaller than swans. Physically, I mean. Swans are very large birds."

The swan honked.

"No offense, Hugh," said the Queen. "Anyway, to the Tower!"

This is the Tower of London.

If you've read the first book of my adventures, *Mac B., Kid Spy #1: Mac Undercover*, or the second, *Mac B., Kid Spy #2: The Impossible Crime*, you already know all about the Tower of London. If you haven't, here's the deal: It's a thousand-year-old fortress where many famous people had their heads chopped off. Today the Queen keeps her jewels there.

Dawn was breaking as we arrived at the Tower of London. Greenish light played on the River Thames. The Queen and I stood on the cobblestones. Atop the walls of the fortress, a soldier raised a flag.

"Look at that flag, Mac. It is the flag of the United Kingdom. The Union Jack."

"Weird name," I said.

"It is not *weird*," said the Queen. "'Union,' because it is the flag of the four countries that make up the United Kingdom. 'Jack' is a nickname. It is a cute thing to call a boy named John, and also a flag."

"OK," I said. "I take it back. Good name."

"The Union Jack combines the flags of England

and Scotland,

and adds a red X from Saint Patrick's Cross, for Northern Ireland."

"What about Wales?" I said.

"Wales didn't make it onto the Jack," said the Queen.

"What!" I said. "A Welsh person would definitely find *that* offensive."

"Mac," said the Queen. "Stop."

"What does the Welsh flag look like?"

"It's a red dragon on a green-and-white field."

"Seriously?" I said. "You should put a dragon on the Jack!"

"Mac, do not tell me what to do with my Jack."

"But it would look cool," I said.

"Mac," said the Queen. "How would you feel if I told you that your mother's boyfriend, Craig, was a nice man deep down, and that you should spend some time bonding with him?"

I frowned. "I would feel like that's none of your business."

"Precisely," said the Queen. "That is how other countries feel when Americans interfere in their affairs."

"But—" I said.

"Silence!" the Queen ordered. She held her pinkie finger up to the air. "Listen, Mac."

I listened.
But I didn't hear anything.
(It was silent.)

"Do you hear that?" the Queen asked.

"No," I said.

"Exactly," said the Queen. "Normally, at this hour, in this place, we would hear croaking, and flapping, and bloodcurdling screaming. Those sounds, Mac, are the sounds ravens make."

"OK," I said.

"Six ravens live at the Tower of London," said the Queen. "Their names are Raven Rhys, Raven Charlie, Raven Merlin, Raven Olivia, Raven Carla, and Raven Tony. They live here, Mac. This is their home. They should be waking up now. But Mac, the Tower's ravens have been abducted!"

RAVEN RHYS

RAVEN MERLIN

RAVEN CHARLIE

RAVEN TONY

RAVEN OLIVIA

RAVEN CARLA

"No!" I said.

"Yes!" said the Queen.

"A birdnapping?" I said.

"A birdnapping!" said the Queen.

"Why would somebody steal a bunch of crows?" I asked.

"A bunch of *ravens*," said the Queen. "Do you know the difference between a crow and a raven?"

"Is this a joke?" I asked.

"It is not a joke! The American crow is smaller than a raven, and it makes a cawing sound, which many people, including me, find brash and tacky. Caw! Caw! Whereas a raven croaks, and has a wonderful vibrato. Like so." The Queen let out a throaty gurgle. "You see? There is nothing funny about it."

"OK," I said.

"Now, Mac." The Queen adjusted her crown. "Do you know why a raven is like a writing desk?"

"Hmmm." I thought for a second. "Well. Hmmm."

The Queen smiled. "*That*," she said, "is a joke! I read it in a book!"

"Oh!" I said. I liked jokes. (I still do.) "Why *is* a raven like a writing desk?"

The Queen frowned.

"I don't know," she said. "The book didn't give

the answer."

"Oh," I said.

"But here is one answer: I would be very upset if someone stole my writing desk, and I am very upset that somebody stole my ravens!"

"That's not very funny," I said.

"Indeed it is not! In fact, it is incredibly serious. These are very important ravens, Mac."

"They are?"

"Yes. I shall tell you a story. In 1667—"

"Oh boy," I said.

"*In 1667,*" said the Queen, "the King of England and his Royal Astronomer were observing the heavens through a telescope, which was installed at the top of the White Tower."

She pointed up at a white tower. (Good name.)

"The King leaned over and peered through the glass, hoping to glimpse a far-off star. But he could see nothing! Ravens were circling the tower, blocking his view, dive-bombing the telescope, and befouling its lens with their leavings."

"Their leavings?" I said.

"Their droppings," said the Queen.

"Their droppings?"

"Don't be crass, Mac."

"I didn't say anything!" I said.

"Now," said the Queen. "The King was furious. He had really wanted to see that star! He shouted down to the guards and ordered all the ravens in the Tower killed. But before the executions could be carried out, the Royal Astronomer stopped the King. 'Your Majesty,' he said, 'it is bad luck to kill a raven.' And then he made this prophecy: 'If the Tower of London ravens are lost or fly away, the Crown will fall, and Britain with it!'"

"Wait, this guy was a scientist?" I said. "He sounds more like a wizard."

"Well," said the Queen, "in those times the line between scientist and wizard was a little blurry. In any case, the King of England declared that from that day forth, six ravens would always live at the Tower of London. And the Royal Astronomer moved his telescopes to a spot a few miles away, where he later discovered Uranus!"

URANUS

"OK," I said.

"Don't be crass."

"I didn't say anything!"

"Mac," said the Queen. "You must recover the Tower's ravens. If you do not, my reign will end! Britain will be lost! We are all counting on you!"

I watched the sunrise.

I thought for a second.

"Your majesty," I said, "that story you told me doesn't make sense. If the King of England was trying to see a star, it would have been nighttime. The ravens wouldn't have been circling the tower. They would have been asleep."

The Queen sighed. "Well, Mac, perhaps it did not happen exactly the way I told it."

"Then how did it happen?"

The Queen sighed again. "Perhaps," she said, "it did not actually happen at all."

"So it's just a story?" I said.

"*Just a story, Mac?* Why then, this thing on my head is just a piece of metal with pointy bits and a bunch of rocks stuck in it. A crown is just a story, Mac. A *Queen* is just a story. A *country* is just a story. People believe stories. Tut tut, Mac! It does not matter whether a soothsayer delivered a prophecy atop that tower. It does not matter whether the King of England actually made a decree. This is a story that every Briton knows. And if the people of this nation discover the Tower's ravens have been stolen, there will be panic. Pandemonium. People will believe Britain will fall, and so Britain will fall. Who cares whether the prophecy is real? The prophecy is true. Do you understand what I am saying?"

"Um," I said. "You want me to find the birds?"

"Yes, Mac. I want you to find the birds."

But I had a question.

"I have a question," I said. "Who would do such a thing? Who would want Britain to fall?"

"That is two questions." said the Queen. "And they are questions you must answer. And quickly. We put a sign at the entrance to the Tower that says 'CLOSED FOR DUSTING,' but people will soon get suspicious. Even the most thorough dusting can only go on for so long. I'd say we have two days. Then all is lost."

A beefeater approached us with a raven on his arm.

"Good morning, Your Majesty," said the soldier.

"Who's that?" I asked.

"This gentleman is the Warder of the Ravens," said the Queen. "His name is Rupert."

"No, the bird," I said.

"Ah," said the Queen. "The bird is Raven George. We keep a backup bird for emergencies like this."

← RAVEN GEORGE

(That's true. You can look it up.)

"Raven George used to live here at the Tower," said the Warder. "But he kept escaping and attacking television aerials."

"What you call TV antennas, we British call aerials!" said the Queen. "Isn't that interesting?"

"I guess," I said.

This is a TV antenna.

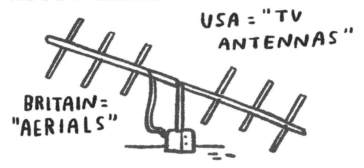

USA = "TV ANTENNAS"

BRITAIN = "AERIALS"

People used to put them on top of their houses if they wanted to get lots of television channels in the 1980s. You don't need an antenna to get lots of channels anymore, but if you check out some rooftops you will probably still see some antennas that have never been taken down, since people generally don't like climbing on top of their houses.

"Raven George destroyed a lot of people's aerials," said the Warder.

"Their antennas," said the Queen. "Or is the plural 'antennae'?"

"He tried to eat them," said the Warder.

"Eating antennae!" said the Queen.

"So he was discharged from service," said the Warder. "Conduct unsatisfactory."

(That's true. You can look it up.)

"He's been living at a zoo in Wales," said the Warder.

The Queen looked at me. "I suppose you would like to make a whale joke now."

I was quiet for a bit.

"I can't really think of one," I said.

"Oh," said the Queen. "In any case, we sent for Raven George this morning. He shall remain at the Tower here while you complete your mission."

"But Your Majesty," I said, "if nobody knows the ravens are missing, why do you need Raven George here?"

The Queen blushed. I had never seen her blush.

"Wait!" I said. "You believe the prophecy?"

The Queen stood up even straighter than she normally did.

"When it comes to the Crown falling," she said, "I am taking no chances. Why, without a Queen, we would be no better than you Americans!"

"Hey!" I said.

"Now," said the Queen, "one of the ravens was wearing a transponder. We picked up the last ping here . . ." She checked a small, tiny computer in her hand. "In Grímsey."

"Grímsey?"

She handed me the computer.

"Where's Grímsey?" I asked.

The Queen shrugged. "How on earth should I know? Look it up."

Grímsey is in Iceland.
This is Iceland.

People will tell you that Iceland is actually green, and Greenland is actually icy, but really Iceland is plenty icy. Look at all this ice:

Iceland even has ice on its flag. Look:

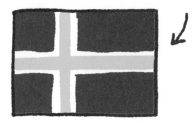

Iceland's flag is a red and white cross on a blue field. The red is for lava. (Iceland has a lot of volcanoes.) The blue is for the ocean. (Iceland is surrounded by the sea.) And the white is for ice. (Told you.)

Here is some lava running past some ice, into the sea, in Iceland:

Wow!

I figured Grímsey was an ice island, where I'd find my suspect's secret spy base, underneath a volcano.

But I was wrong.

Grímsey is flat.

Grímsey is tiny.

More than ten thousand puffins live there.

But only about eighty people do.

There were no volcanoes.

There were no secret bases.

There was, however, quite a bit of ice.

I wished I'd brought a sweatshirt.

A puffin flew by on tiny wings. He looked ridiculous.

But when the puffin turned his head toward me, I realized I also looked ridiculous.

Shivering a little, I went to the exact spot where the raven's transponder had sent its last ping.

It had been a long time since that ping had pinged, but I still hoped I'd find the ravens.

Or at least *some* of the ravens.

I found a chessboard.

That's it.

A stone chessboard, with two stone seats, on the sidewalk, next to a harbor.

"A chessboard," I said. "But does it mean anything?"

Nobody replied. I was all alone. If you want to be a spy, you will often find yourself all alone. Luckily, I was an only child. I was used to talking to myself.

"Mac," I said to myself, "I don't want to break your heart, but I think your mission has reached a dead end."

"Yeah," I said to myself. "I wonder if they have ice cream on this island."

When I was feeling bad, I liked to have some ice cream.

(I still do.)

But before I could tell myself what a great idea I'd just had, someone hit me on the head with something very heavy and knocked me out.

7

KIDNAPPED

When I woke up, I was tied to a chair.

A woman was watching me.

"I have a few questions," I said.

"Me too," said the woman. "That is why I knocked you out and tied you to this chair. But you can go first."

"Thank you," I said. "That's nice."

"We Icelanders are extremely nice," said the woman. "You may ask me three questions."

I didn't think it was very nice to knock me out and tie me to a chair, but I let that go.

"Who are you?" I asked.

"I am the President of Iceland."

"Ah," I said. "Is this room moving, or is that just because I got hit on the head?"

"We are on a boat," said the President of Iceland. "Technically that last question was actually two questions, so you are now out of questions. But I will give you one more, which is extremely Icelandic of me."

"Thanks," I said. "Why does it smell so bad?"

"This is a cod-fishing boat," said the President of Iceland. "It belongs to a fisherman named Willard."

"I'm allergic to cod," I said.

"Well, try not to lick the boat," said the President of Iceland. She paused. "That was a joke."

"I know."

"Now," said the President of Iceland, "let me apologize. We Icelanders are a peaceful people, so I am sorry I had to knock you out. However, it was necessary. And Icelanders are never afraid to do what is necessary."

"It's OK," I said. If you're a spy, you get used to people hitting you on the head. "But why was it necessary?"

"It is my turn to ask questions," said the President of Iceland. "Who are you?"

"My name is Mac B." I said. "I am a secret agent."

The President of Iceland gave me a cold smile. "You have answered your own question."

"Which one?"

"The one about why knocking you out was necessary," said the President of Iceland. "I knocked you out because the Queen of England asked me to."

"WHAT?"

I was so surprised I could have fallen out of my chair, but I was tied to it, so I couldn't.

"That's right," said the President of Iceland. "The Queen of England is a very close friend of mine. She sent me a message—I have it right here."

She pulled out a piece of paper from her pocket and read from it.

Dear MADAM PRESIDENT,

HULLO! As you SURELY remember, you owe me a FAVOR, from when I PICKED you UP FROM the airport that one time. WELL, you can finally pay me BACK. PLEASE go to the ENCLOSED COORDINATES.

They REFER to A spot on GRImSEY which I'M told is in ICELAND. If you find any SNEAKY SECRET Agents LURKing ABOut, PLEASE hit them on the head and KNOCK them out.

The President of Iceland gave me a stern nod. "That's you."

"But!" I said.

"I wasn't finished," said the President of Iceland. She produced a second page.

I just Bought a JET SKI! You should come try it out.

HUGZ,

The Queen of England

P.S. If you find a VERY short AMERICAN LURKing ABOUT, PLEASE REFRAIN from HITTing Him oN the Head and Help him out. He is my SECRET AGENT.

"That's me," I said.

The President gave me a good look.

"I don't think so," she said.

"I'm a short American!"

"Mac doesn't sound like a very American name," said the President. "Max, now *that* is an American name. Or even Matt. Or Willard."

"Willard?"

"Yes! In fact, that spot where I knocked you out, it is a monument to an American Willard! He was a chess player, and he heard that the people of Grímsey were excellent chess players. Of course, Icelanders are generally excellent chess players, but the chess players of Grímsey are especially excellent. So when he died, he left money for a library to be built on this island, and he bought every family on Grímsey a chess set. So that is why there is a stone chessboard in his honor by the harbor. And that is why many parents here, instead of naming their boys Thor, or Gunnar, name them Willard. There are a lot of Willards here on Grímsey!"

(That's all true. You can look it up.)

WILLARD FISKE

"OK," I said. "But still! I am a secret agent for the Queen of England."

"Well this is very odd," said the President of Iceland. "Because I already met the Queen's secret agent at Willard's chessboard this morning. We played a game. I beat him. He was not very tall. And he had a very American name: Johnny Hamburger."

"Excuse me?" I said.

"Johnny P. Hamburger," said the President of Iceland. "The 'P' is for 'Pizza.'"

"Johnny Pizza Hamburger is not an American name," I said. "That is a name somebody makes up when they're trying to think of an American name very fast."

"He was also wearing American blue jeans."

"Hmmm," I said.

"They were very nice jeans. Perfectly faded."

"Can I ask a question?"

"You just did."

"Did he have a bunch of ravens with him?"

"Come to think of it," said the President of Iceland, "he did! Six of them. In a big birdcage. Which, now that you mention it, is very odd."

I wanted to slap my forehead, but I was tied to a chair.

"How did you know?" asked the President of Iceland.

"I'm trying to get those birds back. They were birdnapped from the Tower of London!"

"Oh dear!" said the President of Iceland. "But there is a prophecy—"

"I know!"

"There has been a mix-up!"

"I know!"

"We have to stop that man!"

"I know!"

"Willard!" called the President.

A hatch opened above us. A man with a big beard and a wild sweater stuck his head down belowdeck.

"Oh, hello!" said Willard. "How can I help you, Madam President?"

"Does everyone in Iceland speak English?" I asked.

"Yes," said the President of Iceland. "We learn it from television."

Willard nodded. "Even my boat has one of those, what do you call 'ems, aerials."

"We don't call them that," I said.

"Americans call them TV antennae," said the President of Iceland.

"We call them TV antennas," I said.

"I enjoy watching WrestleFest," Willard said. "Do you love WrestleFest?"

"Joe Brawn!" The President of Iceland flexed. "The American hero!"

"Wrestling is fake," I said.

Willard grinned. "I know!"

"Who cares if it's real?" said the President of Iceland. "It's fun!"

"It's just a bunch of guys tearing off their shirts and throwing chairs at each other."

The President of Iceland grinned. "I know!"

"Hmmm," I said.

"Willard," said the President of Iceland, "where is Johnny Hamburger staying?"

"He's staying out on Willard's old farm. The abandoned place."

"The one with the big blue barn?"

"No, no. You're thinking of Willard's farm. *Willard's* farm, the one by the cliffs. North, past Willard's house."

"Right!" said the President of Iceland. "Come, Mac! There's no time to lose!"

She pulled herself up through the hatch and hurried off.

"Help!" I said.

I was still tied to the chair.

In the saddle on a shaggy horse, I wrapped my
arms tight around the President of Iceland.

We galloped across a grassy plain.

"We are not galloping!" The President of Iceland
shouted to be heard over the wind. "We are tölting!"

"Um," I said. "What?"

"Most horses have four gaits: walk, which is slow;
trot, which is faster; canter, which is even faster; and
gallop, which is the fastest. But an Icelandic horse
has a speed that is even faster than fastest: the tölt!"

We tölted across a grassy plain.

"Tölting is fast!" said the President of Iceland. "Tölting is smooth! It is said you can drink a cup of hot coffee while tölting!"

"I don't drink coffee!" I said.

"Good!" said the President of Iceland. "It can stunt your growth and you are already very short!" She gripped the horse's leather reins. "Tölt, Freyfaxi! Tölt!"

(Freyfaxi was the name of her horse.)

Freyfaxi tölted past farms and tölted through streams. She tölted along steep white cliffs that plunged into the frigid sea.

"There! Willard's place!" The President of Iceland pointed to a shabby shack. Black smoke curled out from its chimney. Johnny P. Hamburger, whoever that *really* was, might still be inside.

"Hurry!" I cried.

"Now," said the President of Iceland, "I have a surprise for you. The Icelandic horse has another gait that's even faster than tölting: Flying speed! Fly, Freyfaxi! Fly!"

Freyfaxi flew. Or at least it felt like she was flying. The president let out a wild cry of joy and shouted, "The Icelandic horse is the best horse in the world!"

The President of Iceland sure bragged a lot.

But to be fair, we were going very fast.

We flew along the ground, beneath puffins flying in the sky, right up to Willard's abandoned shack.

We leapt off Freyfaxi. The President of Iceland pounded on the door.

"Johnny Pizza Hamburger, this is the President of Iceland! Come out with your hands up!"

We stood in the cold for a long while.

"All right, Johnny Hamburger," said the President of Iceland, "we've given you enough time!"

The President of Iceland kicked the door, which splintered and flew off its hinges.

We rushed into the shack.

There was nobody inside, just a small cot, a
rickety desk, and a little iron stove. A few black
feathers floated on a cold draft of air.

"Look!" I pointed to a steaming cup. "It's still hot.
He was just here!"

"Make sure he's not hiding!" said the President
of Iceland.

She checked under the bed.

I crawled beneath the desk.

"He's not down here!" she said.

I didn't find him under the desk either.

But I found something else.

Something that made me gasp!

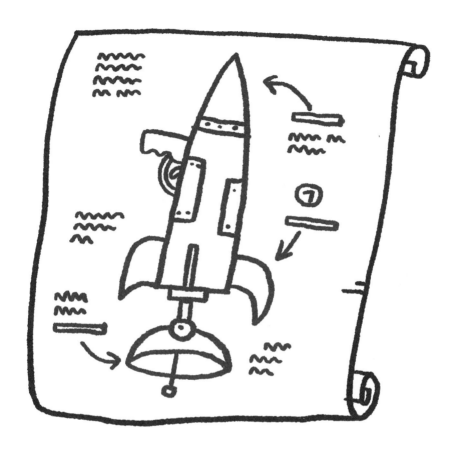

It was a blueprint!

Instructions for building a giant missile, which would probably get fired right at the United Kingdom!

Although I might have been holding the blueprint the wrong way.

I turned it. And I gasped again!

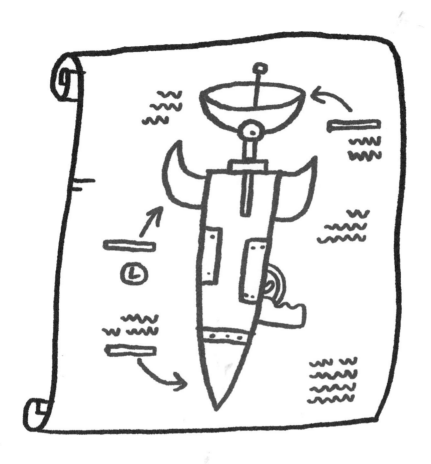

It was a satellite! And it was probably going to aim a powerful laser right at the United Kingdom! From space!

Unless I was still holding it wrong.

I flipped the blueprint.

AND GASPED!

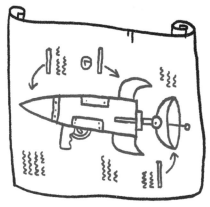

It was definitely a ray gun.

Maybe.

"What are you doing under that desk?" asked the President of Iceland.

"I found something," I said. "A blueprint."

"A blueprint for what?" asked the President of Iceland.

"Um," I said.

Outside, Freyfaxi whinnied.

"Freyfaxi!" cried the president.

We rushed outside and found a man astride our horse, wearing my jeans and no shirt. He held Freyfaxi's reins in his left hand and a birdcage in his right.

I knew that man.

I knew those jeans.

"That's him," said the president. "Johnny Hamburger!"

"His name's not really Johnny Hamburger," I said. "That's the KGB Man."

The KGB Man was my archenemy! He was a spy for the Soviet Union, which was a country in the 1980s. (Most of it became Russia.) And get this: The Soviet Union was Britain's archenemy! The KGB Man created chaos wherever he went. He had stolen the Crown Jewels. He had stolen the Mona Lisa. Plus one time he had beaten me in a karate fight and stolen my pants.

Now this mission was personal.

This was about more than birds.

This was about pants.

"Fools!" said the KGB Man. "You thought you would catch me? I have made you look ridiculous once again!"

"Um," I said, "*you* look ridiculous."

He glanced down at himself. "I look cool!" he said.

"Hmmm," I said.

The KGB Man grabbed the reins with both hands. "Ya!"

Freyfaxi tölted off, carrying the KGB Man straight toward the cliffs.

"My horse!" said the President of Iceland.

"My pants!" I said.

"Also the ravens," I added.

He could not slip away!

"Look!" The President of Iceland pointed.

There was a rusty bike leaning against the shack.

"After him!" cried the president. "He has nowhere to go! He'll be trapped!"

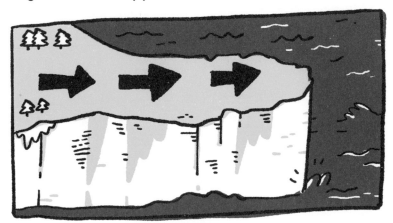

I pedaled hard, bouncing on rocks, jumping over birds' nests, trying to catch up with Freyfaxi.

"Come back here!" I shouted. "Freyfaxi, stop tölting!"

But she tölted on. She tölted hard.

My bike's gears creaked. Its handlebars rattled. I could feel every bump in my bones. I chased the KGB Man toward the edge of the island. Neither of us slowed. Gulls screeched. The wind was cold and salty, and it stung my eyes. But I refused to blink. The end was coming closer. The KGB Man was going to hurtle over the edge of the world, ravens and all, and I would go plummeting right after him.

Freyfaxi neighed and reared up, mere inches from the rocky scarp.

I squeezed the handlebars. The bike's brakes screamed. I slid out of control, throwing a spray of gravel over the edge.

"Stop!" I said. "Halt in the name of the law!"

The KGB Man came tumbling off the horse. He rolled in the grass and leapt onto his feet, and ran over to a camouflage tarp.

"Uh-oh," I said. "I think I know what that is."

The KGB Man gave me a quick sneer before whipping off the tarp to reveal a shiny glider.

"Yeah," I said. "I thought so."

I watched, dismayed, as my archenemy escaped with the ravens. He pushed his beautiful glider off the cliffs and swung into the pilot's seat. He hung the birdcage from a crossbar.

"*Do vstrechi!*" he shouted, waving. "That means 'see you next time'!"

"I figured that's what it meant!" I shouted, shaking my fist at him.

The glider caught a current and rose skyward. A flock of puffins fell into formation behind him. Together they soared gracefully over the raging sea.

"Well, that was cool," said the President of Iceland, coming up beside me.

"It was OK," I said.

I watched the KGB Man escape, willing something to go wrong.

Suddenly, his glider shuddered.

The puffins screeched and scattered.

The glider nosedived. It fell to the sea, tossed about amid the whitecaps.

"Ha! *That* wasn't cool," I said. "What's he going to do now?"

There was a deep rumbling in the water. A gray submarine surfaced, lifting the glider onto its hull. The sub's hatch flipped open, and the KGB Man

hopped out of his glider, skipped across the sub, and popped down into the hole.

It was pretty cool.

"Aw man," I said.

The hatch slammed shut. The submarine turned, pointed north, and dove.

"Where's he going?" I said.

"There's only one place he could be going," said the President of Iceland. "The only thing north of here is the North Pole."

The President of Iceland gave me a ride in her helicopter. We flew to the top of the earth.

The North Pole does not belong to any country, but people from lots of countries have put their country's flag there.

In the 1920s a Norwegian, an Italian, and an American flew an airship over the North Pole.

They dropped the flags of Norway,

Italy,

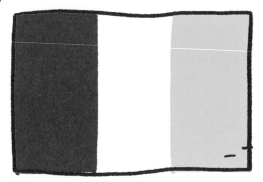

and America

onto the ice.

(Everybody got mad at that Italian because he made sure his flag was bigger than the other two.)

In the 1930s, two Soviets parachuted to the North Pole and put the flag of the Soviet Union in the ice:

And in the 1980s, a Japanese man rode a motorcycle to the North Pole, flying the flag of Japan.

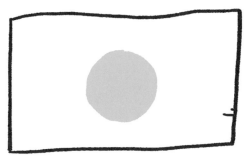

That's true. You can look it up.

The 1980s was also when I landed at the North Pole, in a helicopter flown by the President of Iceland.

We did not plant any flags. I was on a secret mission. As for the President of Iceland: "I will not plant our flag, even though the Icelandic flag is very beautiful," she said. "It is not really our style to plant flags. We Icelanders are a very humble people."

"Um," I said.

"Possibly the most humble," said the President of Iceland, "in the whole entire world."

"OK," I said.

"You must hurry," said the president. "You cannot allow the KGB Man to build that rocket, or satellite, or ray gun, or whatever. His cruel machine. His plan must not succeed! It is a one-two punch!"

"A one-two punch?" I said.

"First he takes the Queen's ravens, then he attacks her with that contraption. It's like when you punch someone—"

She punched me lightly on my arm. When I tried to block it, she punched me harder in the ribs.

"That hurt!" I said.

"I know," said the President of Iceland. "That

was the point. Go! We are all counting on you."

I shivered a little.

"Here," said the President of Iceland, "take this."

She threw down a shaggy sweater. I put it on.

"You look very Icelandic," she said. "That is a huge compliment!"

"Hmmm," I said.

"Good luck!" said the President of Iceland. "I wish I could stick around and help, but I must attend an important meeting about sustainable cod fisheries!"

And with that she flew away.

I didn't know what I'd find at the North Pole.

A bunch of flags?

Elves?

A red-and-white barber's pole?

There was nothing.

I stood in a blank space, alone.

I whipped out my spy binoculars (my mom's bird-watching binoculars used by a spy, me).

When I looked closer, there was plenty to see.
The North Pole was teeming with life!

A walrus.

An arctic fox.

A floating ice base with a Soviet flag on top of
it.

Bingo!

That must be where the KGB Man was building
his rocket, or satellite, or ray gun, or whatever.

Wait. What was that big white bear shape
behind that nice fox?

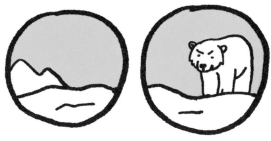

"Oh boy," I said to myself.

That looked like a polar bear. But maybe the ice and snow were playing tricks on my eyes. I blinked and checked again.

"Aw man," I said to myself.

I wiped my spy binoculars, hoping there was just a polar bear–shaped snowflake on the lens.

"AHHH!" I screamed to the freezing void.

It was definitely a polar bear.

And it had gotten very close.

OK, OK.

This was bad.

But I knew a trick! A thing to do when a polar bear is about to attack you!

I remembered reading in a book: You were supposed make yourself look really big and make loud noises!

But then I remembered reading in another book: You were supposed to curl up and play dead.

Those were opposite things!

What was wrong with these books?

What was the point of even looking this stuff up?

The bear roared.

"OK, Mac," I said to myself. "What's it going to be?"

"Look big," I said.

"Or curl up?" I replied.

"Be loud," I suggested.

"Or play dead?" I countered.

I couldn't decide.

I stood there thinking.

I did nothing.

I just stood there (which I think is what you're supposed to do for Tyrannosauruses).

I may be remembering this wrong (because it's hard to believe when I think about it today, years later, in the warmth of my cozy office in California), but I think it licked its lips.

Then it charged across the ice.

"Tell my mother I love her," I said to myself.

"I won't be able to, Mac," I replied. "This bear's going to kill me too."

And then there was barking.

A furious yapping echoing over the snow.

It sounded like a thousand dogs were coming to my rescue!

But there was only one dog.

"Freddie!" I cried.

(Freddie was one of the Queen's corgis. He sometimes joined me on spy missions and he was one of my best friends.)

Freddie tumbled down a snowbank and leapt over a small crevasse.

He slid past me and stood between me and the bear.

The fur on his long back was raised. He bared his teeth and lifted himself to his full height, which was not very tall.

There was an awful moment, a quiet moment, an uncertain moment when anything could have happened, and very few of those things were good.

The bear sniffed once, took a couple of steps forward . . . then turned and ran away.

Wow!

Freddie wagged his tail a couple of times and began licking some ice.

"Freddie!" I cried.

I swept him up in my arms and buried my face in his fur.

He was wearing a little parachute, and there was a note pinned to the pack.

Dear MAC,

I heard you've Been talking to yourself, and so I thought you might Need some company.

You'Re welcome.

The Queen of England

"Come on, Freddie," I said. "We have an ice base to sneak into."

19

THE ICE
BASE

Inside the Soviet base, Freddie and I hid in a barrel of salt cod.

It smelled awful.

Freddie licked some cod.

I did not.

I was allergic to cod.

(I still am.)

We poked our heads out of the top of the barrel and peered out.

Soldiers in uniform were shouting at one another.

Men in masks were welding large pieces of metal together.

A huge wooden crate was being loaded onto the submarine.

The image from the blueprint, whatever it was, was stenciled on the crate, next to Russian letters that I imagined spelled things like "TOP SECRET," "SUPER DESTRUCTO," and "DO NOT TOUCH."

It was the cruel machine.

The KGB Man stood atop the sub, waving the cargo aboard with one hand. He was wearing a sweater. It looked really good with my jeans.

"All right, Freddie," I said. "We have to figure out a way to get onto that submarine, fetch

the ravens, and blow up that machine.

Freddie continued licking the cod.

"Look, I know explosions are dangerous on submarines, but what choice do we have?"

Freddie licked.

It was nice having someone to talk to.

"Shh!" I said. "Quiet, Freddie."

There were voices nearby!

Two soldiers approached our barrel, speaking Russian.

Freddie and I ducked back inside our barrel and eavesdropped on their conversation.

I didn't speak Russian (still don't), and I don't think Freddie did either. But they must have said, "OK, comrade, let's put this barrel of salt cod on the KGB Man's submarine," because that's what they did.

We sat in blackness as the submarine made its journey. I don't know how long we were in there. I was trying to come up with a plan, and also trying not to let any salt cod near my mouth.

"All right, Freddie," I said. "Here's what I have so far. At the perfect moment, you and I will leap out of this barrel and save the day by blowing everything up."

It was dark, so I don't know what Freddie was doing. It sounded like licking.

"Well, I don't know how we'll blow everything up, Freddie," I said. "The KGB Man is bound to have some TNT, OK?"

I nodded.

"Yes, that's the plan. We just wait here for the perfect moment."

More licking sounds.

"The perfect moment, Freddie! The climax, the boiling point, the last second! We will spring forth like snakes from a can, bathed in dramatic glory!"

Someone lifted the lid from the barrel.

I squinted up at the KGB Man.

"Ah. Hello, Mac," he said. He checked his watch. "We still have an hour or so before I achieve victory over the West. I thought I would have a snack. Care to join me in some cod sandwiches?"

"I'm allergic," I said.

"I see," said the KGB Man. "Freddie, you look hungry."

Freddie yipped happily.

We got out of our barrel and joined the KGB Man at a small table.

The birdcage with six ravens hung from the ceiling.

"Where are we going?" I asked.

"You'll see," said the KGB Man.

The submarine surfaced in the River Thames.

Belowdecks, the KGB Man dabbed his face with a napkin.

Freddie licked his plate.

I sat with my arms folded.

The KGB Man pulled down a periscope, took a look, and smiled.

"We are here," he said. "Perhaps you would like to see?"

Trying not to look too eager, I pressed my face against the periscope.

"What?" I said. "What?"

It was the Tower of London.

The KGB Man smiled.

"And now you realize my plan?" he said.

"You're going to . . . give back the ravens?"

"What?" The KGB Man scowled. "No. Why would I do all this just to give back the ravens?"

"Right," I said. "You're going to . . . blow up the Tower Bridge with a ray gun?"

"Nyet. No. There is no such thing as a ray gun."

"With your rocket?"

"Nyet."

"Satellite?"

"Nyet."

"You are going to use your cruel machine!" I said.

"Mac," said the KGB Man, "what are you talking about?"

I took the crumpled blueprint out of my back-pack. (Papers always got crumpled inside my backpack. My teachers hated it.)

"This!" I said.

"Ah!" said the KGB Man. "Cruel machine. I like that."

"The President of Iceland came up with it," I admitted.

"That is not a ray gun," said the KGB Man. "Would you like to see what it is?"

"Yes!" I said. "Duh!"

"Good," said the KGB Man. "It is time to deploy it."

He pressed a button.

The cruel machine rose from the floor.

"Ohhhh," I said.

It was a television aerial.

↖ AERIAL

TV ANTENNA

I mean a TV antenna.

"You're going to capture Raven George!" I cried.

"The last raven," said the KGB Man. "Then I will have them all."

"You fiend!" I said.

Freddie licked the KGB Man's plate.

"You'll never get away with this," I said. "Your plan will never succeed!"

He pressed another button, a red one.

"Commence Phase One," he said.

The top of the sub opened.

I stared as the aerial rose skyward.

"Wait, Phase One?" I said. "There are more phases?"

On the ramparts of the White Tower, Raven George lifted his head.

A gleam in the river had caught his eye.

As a Tower raven, he'd been eating well: rabbit, some blood-covered biscuits, seven grapes, a bit of Brie, and, this morning, a hard-boiled egg. But now it was time for dessert.

He winged his way to the middle of the Thames, making a lazy curve and landing on a deliciously large TV antenna.

Raven George croaked delightedly.

Then a net was thrown over his head.

Now there were seven ravens in the cage.

"Aw man," I said.

But wait!

Ha!

The Tower of London was closed for dusting! Nobody would know Raven George was gone for another day at least! Which meant I had time to return these birds.

"Why are you smiling?" the KGB Man asked.

"Put up your dukes, villain!" I said.

The KGB Man shook his head. "In your story, I am a villain. In my story, I am a hero."

"What?" I said.

"It is like you and your mom's boyfriend, Craig. To you, he is a man who is always hanging around the house, telling you it is not cool to wear pink T-shirts. But to him, you are a smart-mouthed kid who embarrasses him in front of his girlfriend. And then of course, to your mother it is the saddest story of all: You are two people she loves very much but who cannot get along. Whose story is true?"

"Mine," I said.

"There is the problem," said the KGB Man. "We always believe our own stories. The Soviet Union, we are at war with the West. But it is not a war of ray guns. It is a war of stories. You think you are the good guys, and we are the bad guys.

"But in the Soviet Union, we are the good guys, and you are the bad guys.

"That is why my plan is so clever. I will never convince you to believe our story. So I will use your own stories against you. Starting with the story of these birds. When the people of Britain learn I have captured their ravens, they will know we are strong, and they are weak! They will quake in their shoes! The Crown will fall, and Britain with it! I will get a promotion and some nice medals!"

The KGB Man laughed.

"You're forgetting one thing," I said. "Nobody knows these birds are missing."

Now *I* started laughing.

But the KGB Man laughed harder. "You're forgetting one thing. I have a giant TV antenna on top of this submarine. Commence Phase Two."

He pushed a green button and a camera rose up from the floor.

"Aw man," I said.

"Get ready to watch the show," the KGB Man said. "You have the best seat in the house."

I was tied to another chair.

The camera light blinked on.

Freddie was already chewing on my ropes.

(He was a good dog in a pinch.)

The KGB Man looked into the camera and smiled.

"Hello, United Kingdom," he said. "I am an officer in the KGB."

"Hurry, Freddie," I whispered. I could feel the ropes getting looser.

"Perhaps you recognize the birds behind me. They are very famous. Raven Rhys, the cute one; Raven Charlie, the sweet one; Raven Merlin, the cool one; Raven Olivia, the smart one; Raven Carla, the athlete; Raven Tony, the shy one; and my favorite, Raven George, the bad boy. They are the ravens of the Tower of London."

As Freddie gnawed, the ropes frayed.

"But they are not in the Tower of London. They are on my submarine, and we are taking them to the Soviet Union. Britain, we have your ravens!"

Freddie tugged at the ropes.

I strained and twisted, and my wrists broke free!

I had a plan.

"Commence Phase One," I said to myself. "Of one. There's just one phase."

I ran in front of the camera and tore off my sweater.

"What are you doing?" the KGB Man asked.

I tore off my shirt and flexed.

"What are you doing?" he asked again, louder.

"My name is Johnny Hamburger from the USA!"
I said, right into the camera. "Welcome to Wrestle-
Fest!"

"No!" said the KGB Man. "This is real!"

"Yeah!" I said. "Wrestling is real!"

"No! *Nyet!* Really real!"

"Yeah!" I said, flexing some more. "Really real!
You're going down, KGB Man!"

I slapped my elbow a few times, something I'd
seen wrestlers do on TV when Craig was hogging
the remote control.

"Smackdown!" I said.

I jumped onto the KGB Man's back.

He shook me off.

"Pile driver!" I said.

I didn't know what a pile driver was, so I just
jumped on his back again.

The KGB Man stood up and threw me to the floor.

He tore off his shirt.

I scrambled to my feet.

"Sleeper hold!" I said, and slapped my elbow some more.

He picked up his chair.

He was playing right into my hands.

"STOP!" he shouted. "STOP! STOP! STOP!"

He threw the chair.

I ducked.

Something clanged, then something sparked, then something popped.

"My TNT!" cried the KGB Man.

Something exploded.

The camera zapped. Its wires fried.

The submarine was filling with water.

"OK, I guess there's a Phase Two after all," I said. And it was commencing whether I liked it or not.

The water was already to the top of my socks and rising fast.

The KGB Man clambered up a metal ladder.

The birdcage was still swinging from the ceiling.

I looked up the hatch, then back at the birds.

The water was getting so high Freddie had to swim.

(Which was not *that* high, to be honest.)

I could either chase down my nemesis, or save the ravens.

"Come on, Freddie!" I cried.

We saved the ravens.

I stood on top of a quickly sinking submarine with a dog in one arm and a birdcage in the other.

There was no way I could swim while carrying all these animals.

I opened the cage.

"Fly, ravens!" I said. "Fly free!"

Six ravens stayed put.

George fluttered out and landed on the aerial, which was also sinking.

"No . . . just . . . George! That's the wrong direction. Get back in here."

He fixed a beady eye on me and croaked.

I picked him up and stuffed him back in the cage.

There was another blast.

The submarine was on fire in many places.

Downriver, the KGB Man was rowing a dinghy, wearing a fake mustache and my blue jeans.

Freddie was licking my neck.

"Freddie! Stop! I'm trying to think."

A piece of metal came flying and knocked my legs out from under me.

I dropped everything—the dog, the birds—and fell into the river.

I sank.

Time slowed.

The world went green.

Pieces of submarine drifted around me.

Somewhere nearby there was a loud, low boom.

I knew I should swim to the surface—I just didn't
know which way that was.

My ears hurt.

My lungs burned.

I drifted slowly down.

The green got darker.

Some people say there is a river god named Father Thames who lives in the waters that run through London. They say he has lived there for a long, long time. He was there before the Romans . . .

before the Angles and the Saxons . . .

before the Normans . . .

and before the many different people who live in London today.

People say Father Thames has hair like algae and a beard like reeds, that he has watery green eyes that crinkle when he laughs. And if you were ever so unlucky as to drown in the Thames, the kind old face of the river god might be the last thing you see.

People say all these things, and they write them down in books. You can look them up. Of course, that doesn't mean that they're *true*.

But as my body sunk in the murk that day, my chest aching, my vision blurry, I saw the strangest thing: I was about to close my eyes when a smiling face emerged before me.

But it wasn't Father Thames.

It was a dolphin.

No, wait. Actually, it was a porpoise.

And it opened its mouth and grabbed me by
the leg.

The porpoise deposited me on a stone pier, at the feet of the Queen of England.

She was holding Hugh in her arms.

I sputtered and spat up dirty water. The Queen pretended not to notice.

"Thank you, Mr. Nobbins," said the Queen.

"The dolphin's name is Mr. Nobbins?" I asked.

"The *porpoise's* name is whatever I say it is," said the Queen. "And Mr. Nobbins just saved your life.

I looked around. "Where is Freddie?"

"Freddie is fine," said the Queen. "He pushed the birdcage ashore. He is currently licking some cobblestones, but if you call him over, I'm sure he will gladly lick your face."

"Freddie!" I called.

The Queen of England smiled.

"The ravens are back, the sub is sunk, the KGB Man has been foiled again. Anybody watching TV this morning thinks they saw a terrible wrestling program. You seem to have saved the day, Mac, though mostly quite by accident."

I smiled.

"No," I said. "It was on porpoise."

The Queen of England stopped smiling.

Hugh also looked unhappy.

"Mac," said the Queen. "Don't."

When I got home, my mom was happy to see me.

My rabbits did not care one way or the other. Rabbits are not great pets.

Craig seemed like he would prefer that I were not home.

He was watching TV, but I didn't care. I just wanted to go up to my room and get some sleep.

There was a golden envelope on the pillow.

It said:

FOR MAC'S EYES ONLY

I opened it, because I was Mac.

(I still am.)

It was from the Queen of England.

Hullo!

I thought I should write you a "THANK-YOU Note". Thank you. As you apparently ENJOY WRESTLING, I am enclosing a gift: Two tickets to something called WRESTLEFEST LIVE! PERSONALLY, I think it sounds awful, BUT it seems like something you will ENJOY. You may take anyone in the WORLD. FOR instance, CRAIG!

You'RE Welcome,
The Queen of England

I fell back into bed, but before I could shut my eyes, the phone rang.

"Hello?" I said.

"Hullo!"

It was not the Queen of England.

"Is it possible to order cheesy bread without buying a pizza?" a man asked. "Or is that a pizza-only thing? And what in the world is Mountain Dew? Is it what it sounds like?"

"Um," I said.

Someone else picked up and started dialing.

"Hello?" I said.

"Hullo?" said the Prince of Wales.

"Hullo?" asked the Queen of England. "Dear, what are you doing?"

"I'm trying to order a pizza," said the Prince of Wales. "Or rather, I'm trying not to order a pizza and just get some cheesy bread but—"

"This is Mac," I said.

"Mac!" said the Queen. "Just to whom I wished to speak. There is no time for you to thank me for solving your difficulties with Craig. I need a favor."

"I also need a favor," said the Prince of Wales. "Which one of these faucets is cold? Because the water in this tub is very, very hot."

"Dear," said the Queen, "please hang up."

There was a click.

"Mac," said the Queen. "May I tell you a secret?"

I nodded and said, "OK."

Mac Barnett is a *New York Times* bestselling author of children's books and a former ███████████. His books have received awards such as the Caldecott Honor, the E. B. White Read Aloud Award, and the Boston Globe-Horn Book Award. His secret agent work has received awards such as the Medal of ████████████, the Cross of ████████████, and the Royal Order of ████████████ ████████████ the Third. His favorite color is ████████. His favorite food is ████████. He lives in Oakland, California. (That's true. You can look it up.)

Mike Lowery used to get in trouble for doodling in his books, and now he's doing it for a living. His drawings have been in dozens of books for kids and adults, and on everything from greeting cards to food trucks. Mike is the author and illustrator of *Random Illustrated Facts*, and the book *Everything Awesome About Dinosaurs and Other Prehistoric Beasts*, with more Everything Awesome series titles to come. Mike lives in Atlanta, Georgia, with a little German lady and two genius kids.

MAC B.

KID SPY

NEW YORK TIMES BEST SELLERS